Treasured Beach

Chris Sheppard

ISBN: 9798409434663

PublishNation
www.publishnation.co.uk

Darcey,
You're a force, a constant source,
and to me you are my shining light.
It is you who lights up my life.
We have a connection,
a full-blown chemical reaction,
by divine intervention,
you are my shining light.

Chapter 1

Summer

It was the very first second of the very first wake-up of the very first day of the great summer holidays! For most people, it was the best time of the year – apart from Christmas Day. Long days, sun, sea, ice creams, play dates and, best of all, no school!

Darcey was happy about having no school, but she was a little sad, too. She absolutely loved school, just not quite as much as the summer holidays. She was looking forward to all the activities her wonderful mummy had no doubt planned for her.

She opened her eyes and jumped out of bed. She positioned her teddy neatly against her pillow, stood up and stretched her arms into the air, ready for the new day.

This was an important time for Darcey. It was still quiet in her household as she gently opened the draped curtains to let the morning beams of sunshine flood into her room. She had about twenty minutes before her sisters, Harriet and Matilda, woke up. At that point chaos would ensue, therefore Darcey wanted to maximise her time.

She was very organised, and liked to get dressed before leaving her room. Harriet and Matilda, on the other hand, would go down the staircase doing handstands, playing pirate ships – and probably still in their pyjamas!

Today was not only the first day of the school holidays but also the start of the family's summer holiday. This was a big occasion for Darcey and her sisters. It was always fun, and full of adventures and activities. Darcey needed to be organised before they set off.

She started arranging holiday essentials for eight-year-olds across her bed.

Cuddly Bear ✓

Sunglasses ✓

Colouring set ✓

iPad ✓

Activity book from her great aunt, left over from Christmas ✓

Extra pens and pencils, just in case ✓

The family was going to Wales. Darcey was not sure why the country was called Wales because she'd never actually seen a whale there. Looking through her bedroom window, she could see Wales on the other side of the Dee estuary. From her house in Heswall, it looked like nothing more than a giant hill in the distance.

Darcey often peered through her window in the early evening, looking out across to the hills as the sun dropped behind them and often cast a pink hue across the bay. She would reminisce about her summer holidays. She loved spending so much time with her family. She loved the long days playing on the beach, splashing in the sea and exploring new places; she even enjoyed doing arts and crafts on the rainy days that were very common in Wales.

There was a good chance she would see her best friends, Eva and Sophie, who were sometimes there at the same time. Darcey smiled at the thought of all the good times she'd had on holiday in previous years; they more than compensated for the time away from school.

Just then, her door burst open without so much as a knock. 'Darcey,' said Harriet. 'We're going on holiday. We need to get ready right now!'

'Yes, I know, Harriet,' said Darcey. 'I'm ready to go.'

Before she had time to finish her sentence, Harriet was running around the house telling everyone that they were going on holiday today – in fact, right now.

Matilda, the youngest of the sisters, joined in and was swung down the banister rail screeching, 'Holiday!' This was quite a turn of events because, on a normal school day, they were usually quite slow to get ready.

Darcey sat down quietly to finish reading her book by Alice Roberts about the Bronze Age. The chapter was about coastal treasures more than three thousand years old that had been found on the British Isles. She thought this was fascinating, and just the thing to put her in the mood for a trip to the seaside.

She was a very bright young girl. She loved to learn about the world around her and how we all got here. She thought about how people lived near the coast and the many treasures they had left behind – gold, silver, jewellery, axes and many more things – at the same time as the Egyptians were building pyramids in Africa.

'Any last things you want to put in the car?' shouted Mum.

'Hold on!' Darcey grabbed her rucksack, shut her bedroom door behind her and ran downstairs.

The car was always ridiculously full during holiday trips. Every year the children were a little bigger and had more stuff, whilst the car stayed the same size. They were packed like sardines in a tin, only this tin had wheels and they had to sit in it. Sometimes they were in the car for hours and hours, or even a whole day, like when they had made a trip through the mountains of Scotland.

Wales was not such a long distance away, but the car offered the girls less room than a seat on a budget aircraft and that would make for an uncomfortable journey. They were packed in with their toys hanging out of the windows and windbreaks strapped to the roof. There was just about enough room for the dog, Rosie, to squeeze in as well. She would be in the front passenger footwell because there was not one inch of spare space in the car boot.

Darcey jumped into the car. Her seat was covered by a jacket, and there were several bags of holiday necessities packed around it. Frankly, the car looked like a jumble sale on wheels!

She squeezed in and, with one last push, clicked her seat belt in place. She could no longer move; she couldn't even straighten her legs, though she managed to angle them into the least uncomfortable position.

'iPads at the ready,' called Mum.

'Has everyone been to the toilet?' asked Dad. 'I'm not stopping if you haven't.'

Darcey rolled her eyes, knowing full well that he would. And with that, they were off to Wales!

Chapter 2

Travel

'Okay, iPads off, everyone,' said Dad.

That indicated that the children needed to pay attention and observe the scenery. They all looked unimpressed as they reluctantly switched off their tech.

Darcey stared out of the window. She had a bright purple teddy bear's leg obscuring some of her view, but she could make out the mountains. They were blocking out the sun, and the tops of them were dark grey and looked crumbly. Perhaps they were often covered with snow. The lower parts of the mountains were various shades of grey, peppered by white spots which were, of course, sheep. There were several of these mountains all around them, and they made an impressive scene.

Matilda, however, had a better idea and sneakily turned on her iPad again. If she kept it in silent mode, her parents in the front of the car could not see what she was up to!

As the car turned away from the valley and out of the shadow of the mountains, houses appeared to the left and right of the road. Most of them looked a little worse for wear, as if time had forgotten them. Many were noticeably smaller than an average house – even the doors looked child size.

As they drove further down the road towards the coast, the houses became more impressive: painted white, covered in glass and better maintained. At that moment, the sun shone through the window.

'Can you see the sea?' asked Dad.

'I can,' said Harriet. 'What do I get for seeing it first?'

'You get thrown in first,' said Dad.

'No, Daddy,' said Harriet. 'The only person we are allowed to throw into the sea is you. It's your rule.' That was true. It was Dad's way of keeping the children safe.

The car cruised down the coastal road that ran parallel to the sea. They were close to their holiday house and the children perked up.

Darcey caught sight of the sweet shop. Its name, Candy Cane, was in bright pink letters and the whole shop was painted a vivid blue - the sort of blue that made the sea look dull even on a sunny day, which, surprisingly, today was turning out to be. Candy Cane was a dentist's horror show, but the children absolutely loved it. It had wall-to-wall sweets from every era in every colour and every flavour; there must have been more than a million sweets inside that shop. They even had sweets like blackjacks from the olden days when the grownups were children.

'Look at that,' said Dad.

They immediately turned their heads and looked out hopefully. There was a giant rainbow in the distance over the green hills. The sun was bursting through and shining a yellow beam directly onto a length of beach on the far side of the bay. The water glistened and danced in shimmering waves, and the beach was golden in the sun. It was like a distant oasis in a typical British morning that was overcast, with the odd patch of drizzle.

'Wow!' gasped the girls. 'That rainbow is amazing.'

'And can you see the beach?' asked Dad

'Yes, it's golden,' said Matilda.

'That's because it's called Treasure Beach,' answered Dad.

It wasn't, of course. In fact, the narrow stretch of sand wasn't even big enough to have its own name. It was at the edge of one of the many coves in the area and only accessible during low tide.

'Is it made of real gold?' asked Matilda, with the amazement that can only come from a five-year-old.

'No,' said Dad. 'Unfortunately not. However, some people believe that there are gold dragon eggs on that beach. That is why there are all these flags with red dragons above the houses.'

The girls quickly scanned the houses as the car continued down the winding coastal road. To their astonishment, many were displaying flags with dragons on them.

'Right, we're nearly there,' said Mum.

Rosie, the fluffy brown family dog, perked up in anticipation. She had stayed calmly in the footwell for the past hour, but she could sense that freedom and fresh adventures were around the corner. In this instance, she was right. She leapt up onto Mum's knee and sat looking out of the front window with great excitement. In a dog's world, the beach was not something to be taken lightly.

The rocky coast had various bays and inlets full of sand and shells, and when the tide was out there was a sea of brown rubbery seaweed.

The holiday house appeared in the distance – you couldn't miss it.

The house was like no other. For a start, it was about three times the size of any other in the area and, whilst they were all square, white and glass covered, this was like something from the Romanian mountains. It was so pointy, dark and spooky that you expected Count Dracula to live there! He did not, or at least they hoped not. It was built on a giant jagged rock with the sea rushing in from either side. It must have been a ghastly place in the winter.

The car gently pulled up onto the steep driveway. It was at such an angle, they felt like they were about to launch into outer space, or at the very least from the top of a giant rollercoaster.

'We're here,' said Dad. 'Everybody out.'

Chapter 3

Holiday House

Rosie was the first out of the car. She flew out of the door and stretched her whole body in an arc-like sprawl, then turned excitedly as the family slowly appeared from the jumble sale on wheels. A doll, a hairbrush, a half-eaten packet of Quavers and an odd sock had already spilled out of the overflowing car.

The girls grabbed their backpacks, which were filled with all the essentials every small child should have, and ran up the dusty driveway to the front door. It was enormous, raised high upon a step, and seemed to reach all the way to the roof of the house with its many turrets. There was no electric doorbell like at home, no LED flashlight, just one giant round door handle like something a farmer would put through a bull's nose, only bigger.

Mum pushed the open door. It creaked, in keeping with the house, as did the dusty old floorboards. Even ever-enthusiastic Rosie hesitated because of the house's spooky presence.

Once the door was closed, the girls felt more confident. The house was familiar because they had been there several times before. They darted up the winding old wooden staircase to select their beds on a first-come, first-serve basis.

Although the house was enormous, it was all angles and beams. There was height aplenty, but just two rooms between the three girls. The twin room at the front of the house had the advantage of being next to the toilet. However, it was at the front of the house above the front door, and therefore firmly in the shadows. The windows were long and cold to the touch, even in July.

Matilda and Harriet flung open the door and, like Olympian shot-putters, threw their bags onto their respective beds to claim their spaces for the week.

Meanwhile, Darcey calmly made her way to the double room at the front of the house. It was not quite as big, but it had spectacular views across the bay. Large, cobweb-like net curtains drooped down the windows, catching some of the distant sunlight which threw shapes across the wall and highlighted dust particles floating in the air.

Darcey's ever-active mind was still thinking about the beach they had seen earlier. She pulled one of the curtains aside and peered through the window over the bay. The weather had changed; the sun had now broken through and was shining all around, from the tops of the hills in the distance, over the deep blue of the Irish Sea, right the way up the grass-covered cliff tops down the coastal path.

The 'golden beach' was harder to spot in the distance but, after staring at the view for some time, Darcey located it. It did not look so spectacular now that the sun was not highlighting it.

She stared with deep concentration for a moment, looking for any signs of dragons, but she could see nothing. There was the odd white speck that moved swiftly, but that was probably just a seabird. Darcey was looking for something much darker, with scales and claws and giant wings.

Most of all, she wanted to find out if there were really golden dragon eggs on the beach. She would never see them from across the bay because it was just too far. However, the inlet was not far out from the beach where the family often staked a claim.

Darcey knew that dragons probably didn't exist any more, but the thought of golden dragon eggs seemed far more believable. They could have been there for many years – thousands perhaps. That thought was enough to compensate for not seeing a dragon and it ignited her excitement. That would be her mission for tomorrow: go to Treasure Beach in search of golden dragon eggs!

Chapter 4

Beach

It was the first proper day of their holiday, a day of adventure. When they were asked during breakfast what was the first thing they wanted to do, it was a unanimous decision – go to the beach!

The girls loved the beach, where the afternoons seemed to pass in a flash. The very thought of sand, salt water and sun sent them into a dizzy haze. By the end of the day they would be exhausted and too hot, with sand absolutely everywhere, but they would still want to do it all again the next day.

Breakfast – fruit, toast with lashings of strawberry jam and some fresh orange juice to wash it all down – was over almost before it had begun. In fact, it was probably the world record for a family breakfast. Soon the girls had their swimsuits on and buckets, spades and fishing nets in hand, ready for their adventure. After all, it was nearly a whole year since the last time they'd been down to the sea!

After a very short car journey to the car park just up the hill from the beach, the family arrived at their destination. The girls had already spotted a solitary ice-cream van not too far from the beach.

Although they had already guessed what it would sell, they took a long, hard look at the menu as they walked past.

Orange Ice Lolly

Feast!

Milk Lolly

99

Their attention turned to the beach itself as they moved from the hard concrete road to the silky sand. All but Daddy, that was; he was lagging behind, carrying what looked like half the contents of their garage back home. He was peering through the pink fishing net with his head tilted to one side to avoid the spear-shaped legs of the multi-coloured wind break.

'Come on, Daddy,' shouted Harriet. 'We're nearly there.'

The girls ran ahead, eager to see how the beach looked this year. As they approach the isolated rock at its centre, they could see where they usually set up camp when the spot was vacant. They headed straight there.

Matilda immediately sat down and began to dig a beach hole. No beach camp was complete without a beach hole, preferably at least as deep as one of the children.

Harriet ran to the sea to see if there was any sign of life, any movement, anything that she could catch She was quite proficient in the art of catching things with her beach net; she was on record for catching a shrimp nearly the size of a lobster, the scariest-looking scorpion fish anyone had ever seen, a velvet crab with angry purple eyes, and so many varieties of small fish that she could have opened her own aquarium. However, in all instances they were put back safely into the sea. Harriet was a keen ecologist and made sure that everyone around her knew to take only pictures and leave only bubbles.

Darcey, meanwhile, climbed to the top of the central rock and took in all the beach had to offer. The rock was easy to climb from all sides, other than that which faced the sea that had a sort of cavern hollowed out of it.

Matilda had already given up the hard work of digging the beach hole and was cradled in the partially shaded rock cavern, sunning herself and relaxing.

Darcey looked around. She could see half-a-dozen families sitting on the sand. One family of four was standing in a circle, knee-deep in the sea, throwing a bright orange ball to each other.

'Right,' said Daddy at the top of his voice. 'Where are we setting up camp? Right here looks the best place.' He dropped everything on the spot.

The beach ball bounced on his foot and rolled towards the sea. Rosie ran over, grabbed it in her mouth and pounced into the water, looking back at everyone and wagging her tail.

'In a minute, Rosie,' said Mum. She and Daddy constructed the base camp by holding out the windbreak in a circle and hitting one of its legs at a time with a mallet into the forgiving sand. Eventually it was ready, which pleased Darcey very much.

After great deliberation, she shouted down from the rock, 'Does anyone want to build a sandcastle with me?'

'Yes!' shouted her sisters in tandem.

'Daddy?' asked Darcey.

'Yes,' said Daddy, rolling his eyes. What they actually meant was that Daddy could do most of the digging – he'd even brought along a large spade from the garden to help with the project.

Darcey looked at the line of the beach where the sand was wet. It was the ideal spot to make a giant fort or sandcastle. The sand was wet enough to mould, yet dry enough to hold. She pondered whether she could make the construction closer to the sea so that water could be diverted into the structure as the tide went out. The bonus would be that when the tide turned, they could have lots of fun defending the fort against the encroaching tide.

'Here is the best spot,' said Dad.

Darcey was a little disappointed. It did not look as if the fort would have water features. However, her enthusiasm for being chief engineer of the project defeated her disappointment, and she explained to everyone what the fort would look like.

'It will definitely have an enormous wall facing the sea, with turrets at either side and a door in the middle. There will be a moat all the way around that we can fill with water. We need a path into it from the back, too, facing Mummy up the beach.'

'Okay.' Daddy rolled his eyes again at the thought of the hard work ahead, but Darcey was sure he enjoyed it really!

She found a spade and started to dig. Daddy had already created a rough outline, so both Matilda and Harriet started digging too. Matilda tried to place an upturned bucket of sand on top of the wall to create the turret, but the wall was only half built and not flat on the top, so her 'turrets' rolled off and collapsed down the sides.

Darcey's enthusiasm started to wane and her mind drifted to what might lie beyond this beach. She looked at the sand between her toes. It was not as pure as she had expected. It was a mottled colour, made up of yellow, brown, white and even black rather than the golden blanket she had imagined.

The sun had gone in too now and she felt rather cold because of the wet sand beneath her feet. She ran over to Mum and asked what time lunch would be.

'In a minute,' said Mum. 'Has Daddy finished your sandcastle yet? It looks huge – bigger than last year's.'

'Yes, it probably will be,' said Darcey.

'What's the matter?' Mum asked as she dusted yet more sand off the tartan beach blanket.

'I want to go to the other beach. I want to see if there are golden dragon eggs there.'

'You can, but not until you've eaten,' Mum told her.

Soon the family gathered reluctantly for a beach lunch.

'Can we have ice cream?' Matilda demanded.

'After you've eaten lunch,' Mum replied sternly.

A beach lunch comprised of home-made sandwiches wrapped so tightly in clingfilm that they looked like they were about to burst. On the way to the beach they had been squashed from numerous different angles in the cool bag by several frozen packs of juice, which had acted like ball bearings in a pulveriser every time the bag was moved. The only good thing about the packets was that they kept the contents of the bag cold.

Today was turning out to be one of the few British summer days when the sun came out on the beach. The giant yellow sun had worked its way through the last of the morning clouds, and the sky was bright blue. It was so bright that the children knew they shouldn't look directly up at it.

Darcey picked up her juice pack, which was still solid ice inside. She grabbed the nearest sandwich and peeled away the clingfilm very cautiously. The one guarantee about any food eaten on the beach was that it would be full of sand. It got everywhere; no matter how careful you were, it infiltrated and spoiled any meal – especially squashed sandwiches.

Sure enough, with each bite of the very soft bread wrapped around some very soft cheese, Darcey's teeth went crunch! She paused after a couple of bites and looked very carefully at the sandwich; yes, there were little grains of conquering sand all over it. She quickly buried the sandwich in the sand beside her, hoping never to see it again.

'Is it time for ice cream now?' she asked. She was still hungry after only a bite-and-a-half of sand-sandwich.

'Yes, of course,' replied Mummy. 'Come on, let's go.'

The ice-cream van was not far away at the other end of the beach, about the length of two school playgrounds. The children had another burst of enthusiasm because the ice-cream van visit was the highlight of a fantastic day on the beach.

Matilda and Harriet decided to make their way down the beach knee-deep in the sea; that way, they could still have fun and get up to mischief. They were hopping over waves and falling behind the others when a blue ball landed beside them.

Harriet looked around and saw a boy with similar glasses to her own holding out his arms. 'Is this yours?' she asked.

'Yeah. Can you throw it back?'

Harriet gave a great big smile, then launched the ball in his general direction. Before she had time to gauge his reaction to her astonishing throw, Matilda shouted, 'Harriet, come on or we'll get left behind! Mummy and Darcey are nearly at the ice-cream shop.' That was rather an upmarket term for an ice-cream van!

Both girls ran out of the shallows so they could scamper up the beach and catch up. Meanwhile, having noticed several pretty shells, Darcey had slowed down. Following a holiday in Dorset several summers earlier, she had become an avid collector of stones, shells and fossils. She particularly liked the long snail shells that she called 'unicorn horns' because that's what they looked like.

The girls finally reached the ice-cream van and looked at the various stickers splashed across its side advertising what was on offer. Harriet was first to decide. 'I want chocolate – a chocolate cone with extra chocolatey ice cream, chocolate sprinkles, chocolate sauce, and at least two full-size Cadbury's flakes on the top.'

To the children's amazement, Mummy said with a smile, 'Yes, of course, Harriet. Let's make it three flakes. We are on holiday, after all.'

'I want the same, but with strawberry ice cream,' said Matilda.

Darcey shrugged, smiled and said, 'I will just have vanilla with one flake, please.'

The old lady who owned the van had been listening the whole time. She nodded, turned away and busily worked through the order. It always amazed Darcey how many varieties of ice cream could be stored in what was essentially a car, albeit a large car. Before long, the old lady turned around with a fabulous array of ice creams; she had obviously been extra generous with the chocolate sauce and sprinkles!

The girls smiled with glee.

'There you go,' said Mummy.

Harriet exclaimed, 'This is the best day ever, Mummy.'

The family meandered back to their base camp, indulging themselves in their sugary delights before the midday sun made milk shakes out them. For once Mummy could relax knowing that whatever mess the girls made, they could easily wash themselves in the warmish sea.

Chapter 5

Rock pool

'Right, I want to go to Treasure Beach that we saw from the car on the way here. I think it's just around the corner,' said Darcey.

'Okay, but you must stick together and be very careful. Keep away from the deep water, especially if it is moving, and don't go too far,' said Daddy.

'But we need to go as far as it takes to get to the beach,' said Harriet.

'No, not too far – and be careful.'

Harriet rolled her eyes as she stuffed some gluten-free Battenburg cakes in her pocket. 'Okay, Darcey, let's go,' she said.

Darcey was very excited. All morning she had been trying to work out her plan. It was after noon now, the sun was still high in the sky, and the tide was so far out that they could hardly see the sea. On their side of the beach, the water had retreated behind a jagged rock that reached across the cove. The uncovered beach was fairly bare, with a few smooth, sunken rocks and clumps of a brown kelp-like seaweed near the water line.

The girls set off on their journey, excited at what might lay ahead of them on Treasure Beach. They fully expected to find some dragon eggs!

Hopping quickly over the newly exposed sand, they reached the rock that had been obscuring their view all morning. Around its base were

40

several sunken, sandy hollows with little rocky islands dotted around them. They were covered almost from top to toe in the brown seaweed.

Harriet was on full alert for any moving critters. She had brought along a fish net and bucket, as well as her pocket full of Battenberg cake. 'I've seen a giant crab,' she said. 'Wait, and I'll catch it.' She moved quickly to a rock and stood over it like a heron, watching carefully.

'It's there! I see it, it has red eyes.' As Harriet swooped her net towards the crab, it darted under the seaweed at the base of the rock. It was now under water, so Harriet waded in until she was knee deep and prodded the bottom of the rock with her net. Three or four shrimps darted out, but there was no sign of the red-eyed crab. By now, it had nestled firmly under the rock.

Harriet worked carefully, prodding with her net. The crab made a dash for it – it was much quicker than she expected. It ran across to the edge of the rock pool, across the sandy shore and onto the rocky outlet.

'There it is!' said Darcey.

As Harriet waded out of the pool, Matilda darted after the crab.

'Where did it go?' Darcey asked, having caught up with her sister.

'It went in there. I saw it climb up the rock and run through this hole.'

Matilda was right. There was a hole the shape and size of a rugby ball in the rocky outlet, ideal for escaping crabs. The girls gathered around to look, though they didn't want to get too close. They were on guard in case the crab, or anything else for that matter, wanted to come out.

It was very dark inside the hole. The dark-grey rock glistened with sea spray, and several snails were grouped together in one corner. The girls squeezed tighter together to look.

Inside was a bath-tub sized rock pool full of life. The girls realised they would get a better view from the other side of the large rock so, one by one, they ran around the furthest point of the rock to see what was in the pool.

Darcey was first, and she crouched down and peered into the pool. Harriet and Matilda swiftly joined her. They could see the rugby-sized hole at the other end of the pool that the crab had run through. Light shone through it, illuminating the still water.

The pool stood so calmly in its very own rocky shelter, tucked away from much of the hustle of beach life.

As the girls looked down, it was just like viewing an aquarium. Their eyes adjusted to the light, and the true magic of the rock pool became clear. There were bright-red, mushroom-like anemones, lush sea grass, and soft-orange corals standing proudly among the gentler greens and browns that carpeted the floor.

As the girls sat still, small shrimps busily fumbled at everything within reach.

'There it is,' exclaimed Harriet, pointing to the darkest corner of the pool. 'You can see its red eyes glaring.'

'Oh yes, just like a dragon!' said Matilda, having set out on the expedition hoping to finally see a real dragon.

The crab cautiously shuffled backwards until it was snug within a rocky crevice, and neatly folded in its arms and legs. The girls stared for a moment, waiting for its next move.

A few seconds passed before a rock goby swam along the bottom from the shadows to catch a beam of light across the water. It also paused on the sandy bottom.

Darcey was kneeling, so her feet were behind her. She suddenly noticed that they were covered with water because the tide was slowly creeping back in.

'Look, the tide is coming in. Let's leave the crab and his friends,' she said.

Harriet was keen to catch the crab, but she realised that her older sister was being sensible. Anyway, Matilda really wanted to see the dragon too, so they agreed to move on.

Chapter 6

Friends

Matilda walked on ahead. As they looked down the shoreline, now that they had passed the rocky inlet, they had a clear view out to sea. It was still very calm and there were a couple of large boats on the horizon.

They knew that Treasure Beach was just a little further around one more corner. The water was ankle deep now and slowly rising. Most of the water was covered in seaweed that danced up and down as the waves came gently in and out. The water was very clear and the yellow sand beneath it was bright against the brown wall of seaweed.

A few small fish moved around, darting away when the girls approached.

The rocky wall to their left was fairly steep, with seaweed as high as their waists. They assumed that was the level the water would rise to. Beyond that was an array of snails and limpets.

It was far too steep to climb, even for Harriet, so the girls carefully edged their way further into the water.

'I'm not sure this is a clever idea,' said Darcey. 'I think it's too deep.'

'I can't climb that wall,' said Harriet. 'Even if I did, I need the two of you to get up there, too.'

'We will have to go back,' said Darcey.

All three of them were extremely disappointed. The time they had spent marvelling at the wonders of the rock pool had stopped them from reaching Treasure Beach and any possibility of seeing dragons.

Just then, a blue-and-yellow inflatable boat pulled up beside them. 'Ahoy there, me matey,' a voice shouted from on board. It was Darcey's friend from school, Eva.

'Hey, Darce,' said another voice that seemed to come from nowhere. A head wearing a snorkel popped up behind the boat; it was Sophie, another of Darcey's school friends. She was wearing fins and had been swimming behind the boat to propel it.

'Oh, hi!' said Darcey excitedly. 'I didn't expect to see you guys here today. Are you on holiday?'

'Yes, we are. We only arrived about ten minutes ago,' said Eva. 'Your mum said that you're on an adventure to find some dragon eggs on Treasure Beach.'

Harriet butted in. 'Well, we were but we can't get around the corner now because the water is too deep.'

'Jump in, then,' said Sophie. 'We can get further with this boat. I can easily swim behind – just tell me when to stop.'

With little hesitation, the girls agreed and climbed into the boat, ready to set sail – or, in this case, instruct Sophie to kick, which she did rather elegantly.

The boat moved forward. 'Hold on, its sinking!' cried Eva.

It was indeed struggling to stay afloat. The girls had been so excited to see their friends and finally have a chance to get to Treasure Beach, they had forgotten that the boat couldn't take four people. Their weight was allowing the gentle waves to splash over and fill the boat at an alarming rate!

Darcey reacted quickly and jumped out of the boat beside Sophie. She clung on to the rope that went all the way around the side of the boat. Thankfully, the water was still only waist deep.

'Phew, that was scary,' said Matilda.

'It's okay now,' Darcey reassured her. 'I'll swim behind with Sophie. Eva, can you tell us which way to push?'

The girls glided over the water, past the snail-laden rock, towards the golden beach that lay ahead. The seaweed gently stroked Darcey's legs as she kicked at the back of the boat. It was a strange sensation at first, and some of the longer strands clung to her for a moment. However, before too long both Darcey and Sophie had become accustomed to its friendly touch as they edged closer to the beach.

Sophie's arms were outstretched as she pushed the boat along. Her head was in the water as she watched the bottom. Suddenly she jumped up and raised her arms in the air. 'Stop! Stop!' she cried.

Alarmed, everyone in the boat turned around and looked at her. At that moment, Sophie pivoted and her legs pointed into the air before she slowly sank before their very eyes! After a few seconds, she reappeared with what looked like a giant red monster in her hand. It waved it legs before clasping Sophie's arm like a sloth on a tree.

'What on earth is that? Is it hurting you?' Matilda asked with a shocked look on her face.

Sophie smiled. 'No, of course not. It's just a friendly spider crab.'

With a disgusted look on her face, Matilda replied, 'I dislike spiders.'

The other girls burst out laughing.

'It's not a spider, Matilda, it's just a giant crab,' Darcey smiled.

Sophie took a good look at the handsome, leggy beast before dropping him back into the ocean to continue with his mission, whatever that was. The girls continued with theirs, too.

'Nearly there,' shouted Eva.

'Aye, aye, captain,' shouted Darcey. She and Sophie kicked eagerly to speed up their arrival.

Sitting on the boat's bow, Matilda and Harriet were already scanning the sprawling beach for any signs of dragons, dragon eggs, or anything else exciting.

Whilst kicking through the water with two hands on the back of the boat, Darcey's knee caught the soft sandy bottom and she knew they had finally arrived. She put down both knees carefully on the sand and looked up over the back of the boat.

Finally she had a close-up view of Treasure Beach, which she had seen just a day ago from the holiday house.

Chapter 7

Treasure Beach

Darcey stood up in the warm water. Her feet sank until she could feel the sand against her ankles. The beach was just as golden as she had imagined, with barely a blemish to be seen.

It was narrow, not much wider than the school hall, but very long. To the left was a grey stone wall that jutted out at different angles, creating small caves, overhangs and possible climbing routes. The rocks were covered by a variety of grasses, and stunning pink sea thrift swayed in the gentlest of sea breezes. The sun was still blazing, bringing out the magic of the beach.

Matilda and Harriet had already jumped out of the boat onto the beach. They grabbed the first things that caught their eye: for Harriet, that was a mermaid's purse, whilst Matilda pulled a giant razor-clam shell from the water's edge.

'Look what I've found,' said Harriet. 'A mermaid's purse.'

'But it doesn't have any genuine treasure in it, does it?' Eva replied.

Harriet looked closely at the mermaid's purse, also known as a shark's egg, and shook her head in disappointment.

Sophie was still kneeling in the water to keep warm. 'Right, everyone. Eva and I need to head back,' she called from the back of the boat.

'What, already? Why?' Darcey looked unimpressed.

'We haven't had lunch yet, so our mums said we could come and say hello but then we have to go back,' Eva explained.

'Oh, I see. Well, we're going to stay here and look for dragons and treasure,' said Harriet, still feeling as enthusiastic as she had earlier in the day.

Sophie was still kneeling beside the boat and she spun it around. On Eva's command, she kicked fiercely, and sand clouded the shallow water before the inflatable boat started to move forward.

The sisters waved eagerly, but it was not long before the boat was out of sight. They looked at each other. 'Right, let's start searching,' said Darcey.

Matilda was slightly hesitant. The realisation that there might be dragons nearby made her move a little closer to Darcey.

Just then, Harriet noted something large in the sky. The sun reflected harshly off her glasses for a moment. 'What's that? she asked.

Darcey and Matilda looked up into the blue sky as a large object with giant wings wider than their car, soared over the cliff tops. It had huge scaley feet with talons on them.

The girls gasped. Matilda jumped behind Darcey and cried, 'It's a dragon and I don't like it!'

Darcey continued looking. She could see that the creature had big white feathers around it is head, making it look rather mythical as it soared in the bright sunshine. Although she had not seen an actual dragon before, she was not sure they had feathers. However, she remembered that dinosaurs had both feathers and scales, so maybe dragons did too.

For a moment some of Matilda's fear affected her, then she noticed its bright yellow beak. That looked familiar, and it reassured her that she was not about to be carried off for lunch. 'It's okay, Matilda. That's not a dragon, it's a sea eagle!' she explained.

Matilda raised her head, which was buried in Darcey's back, and looked up. Yes, it was unmistakably a sea eagle like the ones they had seen on their recent holiday in Scotland. They would never forget that holiday for both the drive and the size of the sea eagle; it was the biggest bird they had ever seen, even bigger than the ones at Chester Zoo!

The bird had already seen the girls on what was normally quite a secluded beach and it turned towards the sea. Using its huge wings, it flapped and gained height. Before too long, it was just a small dot in the distance and then it disappeared behind the distant cliffs.

The girls turned away and started scouring the beach. Matilda, still a little nervous despite the sea eagle's disappearance, stayed close to Darcey. They walked slowly to the water's edge, looking carefully at the ground. The sand was littered with beautiful shells, some of them with a pearl-like glow.

Harriet spotted something golden and glistening. Excited, she ran to it, reached out and picked it up for closer inspection. 'Sea glass,' she shouted.

She was quite pleased with her find because on a normal beach hunt amber sea glass would be one of the rarest treasures. The order of value for sea glass is opaque, green, blue, amber and then red, with the latter two being quite rare.

Darcey and Matilda looked less impressed. They hadn't made all this effort just to find sea glass!

The girls continued searching. Before too long, they had combed most of the shoreline. They each had a pocket full of beautiful shells, and they'd also found several cuttlefish and a few collectable pieces of sea glass – but there was no sign of any treasure.

They moved onto the main beach, which was as pristine as any beach they had ever seen. Harriet walked ahead eagerly. Suddenly she said, 'Look at this.'

Darcey and Matilda looked down. 'It's a piece of seaweed,' said Matilda.

'But it's an X!' replied Harriet, slightly annoyed at having to explain herself. 'X marks the spot!'

Darcey examined it but was not convinced. 'I think it's just a piece of seaweed, Harriet.'

Harriet was very annoyed. She bent down, moved the seaweed to one side and started to dig. Before too long, she had a sizeable hole – but there was nothing in it.

Matilda decided that digging a hole was a good way to find treasure. She had a better idea of where to dig, but she also had no success.

Darcey sighed as she looked at the beach. It was as beautiful as she had imagined, but it didn't have the magical dragons and treasure she had hoped for.

She looked at her two sisters, who by now had made several holes. It was still hot, and they were both covered in sand. 'Girls, I don't think this is any good,' she said. 'We're not going to find any treasure digging like this.'

'No,' agreed Matilda. 'And I'm hot and tired.'

Chapter 8

Discovery

They sat down near the rocky wall of the beach. After being exposed to the scorching sun for most of the day, the smooth grey rock was quite warm. The air was hot and dry, and the children were covered from head to toe in sand. Worst of all, they had found absolutely no treasure.

Matilda said, 'Maybe pirates have been and taken it all. There's a big boat out there.' She pointed out to sea.

Darcey looked and saw a large square tanker sitting on the horizon. 'Oh Matilda,' she said.

'That's not a pirate ship.' She secretly wished that it was.

'Let's have a drink,' said Harriet, pulling a Capri Sun from her bottomless pockets.

Darcey had a quick sip of the refreshing juice. It had been in the cold bag until just before lunch and was still frozen from the night before. She stood up and passed the drink to her sisters before turning despondently and slowly walking away with her head down. She was disappointed. As beautiful as the beach was, there was nothing magical about it. There were no dragons, dragon eggs or golden treasure.

The sun was glaring up above. The rock formations on the cliff had created a partial cave-like structure. Darcey strode to her left and perched carefully inside it on a rocky side wall. She looked back down the beach towards her sisters. The cave hid her from them, but she caught sight of Harriet still eagerly looking for treasure. She sighed, knowing that such a belief was bliss but they would probably return from their adventure with nothing but pockets full of shells, something they did all the time when they walked down Heswall beach with Rosie.

A sense of responsibility and worry crept over her. Their parents would be looking for them. No doubt Mummy would have a reserve bag of drinks, snacks and everything else they needed, but at the moment there was only her and her two younger sisters.

The rock wall inside the cave was very dry; clearly the tide rarely came this far into it. It had a triangular entrance, with the sides almost meeting at the bottom, and its roof was very high.

Sunlight struggled to reach the back of the cave, so it was very dark.

Darcey was not overly keen on the idea of going further, but her inquisitive nature overrode her fears and she moved tentatively inside. The bottom of the cave was not very wide and covered in firm sand. The walls looked bare, though it was hard to see in the low light.

Eventually Darcy's fears overwhelmed her and stopped her in her tracks. As she turned towards the light at the cave exit, to her amazement she noticed a glint on the cave floor. She moved swiftly towards it and knelt for a closer look. She had definitely found something and wanted to see exactly what it was.

It was partly buried but she could see it was golden in colour and had some beautiful patterns on it. Her excitement grew. 'Girls, come quickly! I've found something!' she shouted.

After a few seconds, both of her sisters appeared at the cave entrance.

'What is it?' cried Matilda. 'What can you see?'

'I'm not sure but I think it is something wonderful,' replied Darcey. 'I was looking in here and noticed it on the floor. It's still partly buried in the sand. Look.'

Matilda and Harriet moved closer.

'It is real treasure!' exclaimed Harriet. 'Let me pull it out.'

'No, Harriet, wait.' Darcey recalled the many hours of Alice Roberts' television programmes she had watched at home with her daddy. 'We need to be careful. Let's be gentle.'

Slowly she moved some of the sand from around the piece. It was definitely treasure – it looked like a golden bracelet. It was quite dirty and looked like it had been there for a very long time. She put the bracelet on the palm of her hand. 'Let's take it to the light and examine it.'

She walked out of the cave onto the beach and let the sun shine down upon their newfound treasure. Her sisters eagerly scurried after her.

The bracelet was covered in brown and green dirt that obscured its beauty. Darcey rubbed one edge between her fingers and released its golden hue. It had a train-track pattern around both edges and the centre was covered in stunning circular patterns.

The girls jumped back and gasped in awe at their find. Darcey's eyes lit up and a smile crossed her face. They had finally found some real treasure!

Chapter 9

Seagullosaurus

Once they had calmed down, the girls sat on a rock at the edge of the beach. They noticed that the tide had moved in still further and wondered how on earth they would make it back to their parents.

The reality of their marvellous find was still settling in. Darcey was busy thinking about exactly what it was. It did not look new – but exactly how old was it and who did it belong too, she pondered, whilst listening to the gentle sea breeze.

Matilda broke the silence with a cry of, 'I'm hungry.'

Harriet, of course, had just the thing. She rummaged around in her deep pockets, now overflowing with shells and other beach collectables, before pulling out a whole packet of three mini-Battenburg cakes. She placed them proudly one by one onto the rock where they were sitting. They would give the sugary rush of energy the girls needed after their exhilarating find, just enough to fuel their journey home.

Darcey carefully put the invaluable treasure high onto the rock behind them so it would not be knocked off accidentally, then looked at the marvellous cakes. Her mouth was watering! But no sooner had she decided which one to take when they we interrupted by a sudden, unnerving noise that disturbed the tranquil beach.

The girls were startled by the racket. They looked up and saw a mass of feathers so great that it was partly blotting out the sun. A flock of incredibly angry and hungry seagullosauruses descended upon the girls, intent on getting the cakes!

Harriet grabbed her Battenburg and put it safely in her pocket. Darcey, who was just about to pick up her cake, was shocked as one of the noisier birds swooped down onto the rock they were sitting on. It balanced with its outstretched wings and hopped towards them, then lowered its neck before grabbing hold of a cake. It threw it into the air and flipped back its head. To the girl's astonishment, it opened its mouth and the cake vanished into its gullet as it swallowed it whole, including the packet. After a giant gulp, the bird steadied itself and eyed up the second cake.

Another gull dropped onto the rock, paused and then squawked angrily at the gull that was still digesting the first cake. This gull, who was ready to claim ownership of the second cake having experienced the delights of the first one, squawked back. After a quick, loud interchange, both birds reached to grab the cake simultaneously and flung it into the air. Darcey and Harriet looked on in shock at such aggression.

Just as all seemed lost, Matilda stepped in. She jumped forward and plucked the cake from mid-air with one hand before landing on the rock, perfectly balanced like a world-class ballet dancer. She was in between the squabbling birds, which both looked at her aghast. Rage built up in their tiny little eyes. It became more and more intense until they looked as though they were ready to burst before lunging forward to attack

Matilda and retrieve the cake that they now believed was theirs.

Thankfully, Matilda was proficient in karate as well as ballet – she had watched *The Karate Kid* many times. She instantly raised her forearm to stop one of the approaching birds, before pivoting and performing a sweep kick that knocked it off its feet.

The seagullosaurus was dizzy from the hot sun and full of glutinous cake. It tumbled off the rock with a crash, losing feathers everywhere. Its former adversary saw its chance and lunged at Matilda. She leaned back elegantly so that it shot past her, then she performed a swift hand chop across the angry bird's beak and knocked it to the ground.

The other birds, which had been circling above in the hope of scavenging some cakey spoils, thought better of it and took off as fast as they had arrived. Matilda, still with the Battenburg in her hand, turned to face the remaining birds, even though they were nearly the same size as her. They raised their enormous wings, before they started to move back.

Harriet ran over and shouted at the top of her voice, 'Go away! Go away!'

The giant birds ran down the beach before launching themselves into the air, flapping urgently to get away.

Harriet turned to Matilda. 'That was amazing. I thought for a moment that they were going to eat us all up!'

'They got all but one cake, though – and I'm still hungry,' replied Matilda.

Harriet smiled and reached into her pocket. 'I still have mine.' She showed off her cake proudly.

'Well done, Harriet,' said Darcey. 'We can share these two cakes between us, before those hungry seagullosauruses return!'

Like all good sisters, they shared out the cakes and gobbled them up. Now they were ready for the journey back.

Darcey turned to pick up the golden treasure she had carefully left on the rock behind them – but it wasn't there. Alarmed, she cried, 'Where is it? Where is the bracelet?'

'I don't know,' replied Matilda. 'I thought you had it.'

'I put it up on this rocky shelf whilst we had something to eat. Maybe it was knocked off in all the commotion,' said Darcey.

Chapter 10

Detective

The girls searched the beach, looking for the wonderful treasure. Matilda walked up and down the water's edge; the sea seemed to be closer than when they had arrived, and the long beach was becoming narrower by the minute. All she found were more shells, but her pockets were already bursting with them.

Harriet, meanwhile, had started looking on the rock face. It was a sort of cliff, just not quite big enough to be *called* a cliff. Nor, despite first impressions, was it very steep, and it was littered with different plants and flowers that clung to every crack and crevice.

She climbed up to the very top , something she had done many times on a climbing wall back home. From the top she could see across several fields that were covered in semi-scorched, spindly grass and gorse bushes, which were beautiful and summery with their numerous yellow flowers. She knew they were covered with sharp thorns, so she took good care to avoid them as she worked her way along the cliff. She was also careful not to get too close to the edge.

Harriet had a terrific view of the beach below her where her two sisters were searching. From above, it looked rather desolate. She looked out to the sea, then back across the fields. There was nothing but a rather weary-looking wooden fence, that had certainly seen better days, and a weathered tree in the distance obscuring her view.

Turning away, Harriet remembered the job at hand: to find the missing treasure. For the next few minutes, she paced up and down the cliff edge, but she saw nothing more than a large clam that she assumed the birds had brought up here to feast upon.

She worked her way carefully back down. The rocky slope gave her natural pathways, filled with organic matter that helped her remain sure-footed.

When she reached her sisters, she said, 'I think the seagullosauruses must have taken the treasure when they attacked us. I've looked all over the top of the cliff and found nothing, nothing at all.'

Darcey was very despondent. She had dreamt of finding some real treasure for so long and now that she finally had, it had gone. She would never see it again. To make matters worse, it was all her own fault. She sat cross-legged on the dry sand and sobbed. If only she had done something differently; if only she had put the bracelet in her pocket or kept it firmly in her hand.

Harriet came across and cuddled her. For a moment, she held her sister tightly and reassured her, even though it was difficult to know what to say. She knew how much finding treasure meant to Darcey. To have lost it was worse than not finding at all.

After a short time, Darcey had no more tears and she started to accept what had happened. She opened her eyes and let in the afternoon sunlight; it was so bright that it made her squint.

With her eyes half closed to keep out most of the sun, she peered over to where the bracelet should have been. It still wasn't there. She turned her head away to bury it in her sister Harriet's shoulder. As she did, she caught a flash electric blue, like a fleeting glimpse of a kingfisher passing through. What looked like a bright blue feather was lying on the ground, near where she had lost the precious bracelet.

She quickly stood up and moved over to it. It looked as if it had just been plucked from a bird's bottom! There were several other feathers dotted around from all the pandemonium earlier, but they were white and grey, and large and oily from the sea birds. This one was only as long as her index finger, and it was neat, crisp and unquestionably electric blue.

'That's amazing,' said Matilda, having hurried over. 'What is it from?'

Darcey thought for a moment. 'It's not from a seagullosaurus, that's for sure. In fact, there aren't too many birds that have feathers like this. It's far too big to be a kingfisher – and anyway, I don't think they live near the sea. I've never seen anything like it on a David Attenborough programme.'

Harriet perked up. *She* had seen a bird with such magical electric-blue feathers on a walk down to the beach with Daddy. 'It's from a blue jay.'

Darcey thought for a moment and carefully digested the claim. She joined the dots and solved not only the source of the feather, but also the whereabouts of the shiny bracelet! 'That's it, Harriet, that's it!' she cried.

Harriet smiled. She'd shown her wonder for the natural world, though she hadn't quite realised the full extent of their discovery.

'The blue jay will have taken the bracelet. They're part of the crow family and they love shiny things. It will be collecting them. We must find it and get it back!' Darcey sounded determined and full with hope.

At that moment, the tide rolled gently towards their feet, tumbling various shells and debris as it came. It was about halfway across the beach from when they had initially landed; the tide had well and truly turned and the sea was rushing in. There was absolutely no chance of going back in it to get back to their parents, and no sign of any boats to help them.

Thankfully, the girls knew they could scale the cliff quite easily. Harriet, having already completed the task earlier, led the way.

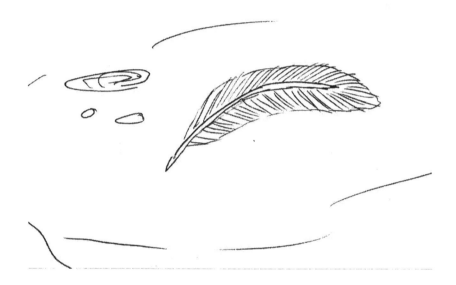

Chapter 11

Blue Jay

It took far longer than expected to scale the cliff, despite it being relatively small. Darcey was so excited that she lacked concentration and became nervous, which, in turn, unsettled Matilda. They clung to the vegetation and stayed low to the ground as they climbed. To Harriet's relief, they eventually made it to the top and got their first view of the landscape.

Matilda noticed that the hard, dry cliff tops were peppered with rabbit droppings and immediately decided against exploring. Harriet had also seen them – and she began to investigate the immediate vicinity for signs of burrows!

Darcey was focused on the task at hand. They were extremely high up now and exposed to the elements. There was hardly a tree for as far as the eye could see. The alpine-green gorse with its buttercup-like flowers was windswept.

In the distance towards the sea, which looked motionless on the horizon, she notice an elongated shape. She walked down the coastal path towards the dilapidated wooden fence and, with great care, peered over the edge. There it was: a solitary tree amid a sea of thorny gorse, with a backdrop of the ocean. It was not the biggest or strongest looking tree; indeed, it looked very sad and malnourished as it stood at the bottom of a rocky embankment that led out to sea.

Matilda ran up behind her. 'Have you found the jay?' she asked.

Darcey was a little annoyed at the interruption because she was still working out the situation. 'Not yet, but that's the only tree around here and blue jays love trees. Look.'

She pointed. Halfway up the tree, on one of the few sturdy branches, sat a well-kept bird's nest. That must be it, she thought to herself.

'Let's investigate,' she exclaimed, marching off towards a stile that was situated a little further down. A yellow sign to the right of it said 'Warning. Falling Cliffs'.

Darcey jumped onto the stile, over the fence and onto the path that descended at the other side without a second thought. If there was any chance of recovering her treasure, she was going to try.

The rocky embankment was dotted with burrows but, from the rabbit and bird droppings on the ground, it was unclear who they belonged to. Darcey loved puffins with their technicoloured bills, but they had long since fled the nest and would be out at sea.

She moved towards the tree with Harriet and Matilda not far behind her. The path was narrow, and numerous plants that could survive the salty sea air competed for space on it. The girls struggled through until eventually they came to the base of the tree.

Close up, it looked older than the pear tree back home in the girls' garden. Its bark was knotted by years of branches breaking off, but there was also new growth. The tree made a shadow down the rest of the embankment.

Darcey looked up at the nest. It was nearly as big as the tree, and much wider than the branch it sat upon. The thick twigs made it hard to see from underneath what was inside it.

'Do you think the blue jay is in there?' asked Darcey.

'Maybe. But how do we know? Will it attack us like those birds earlier?' asked Harriet warily.

'Boo!' Matilda shouted at the top of her voice, to everyone's surprise. Immediately there was the unmistakable flash of electric blue as the jay jumped out of the nest. In a flash, it swooped over the gorse, up the hill and over the fence where the girls had come from.

'There, there!' shouted Harriet excitedly. 'We've found the blue jay!'

Darcey immediately responded, 'But we don't want the blue jay, Harriet. We want our golden treasure back! How can we get all the way up there to look in the nest? It is far too high for us.'

It *was* too high. The girls knew they couldn't damage the nest in any way or risk harming the bird.

Harriet noticed a large branch that had snapped off during one of the frequent storms that the tree had been exposed too. 'Help me with this,' she said. 'Lean it up against the middle of the tree.'

Part way up, the tree had split into two trunks. The girls put the broken branch up against the place where it had split and made sure it was secure.

'Right, I can climb that and look into the nest,' said Harriet.

She carefully placed a foot on the branch and pressed down hard to see if it could take her weight. She didn't weigh much so, although it bounced a little, it held firmly enough. She tiptoed across to the trunk of the tree and held it tightly. Once she was confident that she was safe, she looked down into the nest.

There it was, lying in the nest – the treasured bracelet that the girls had found earlier on in the day! 'It's here, I can see it!' Harriet shouted.

'Can you reach it?' asked Darcey. Her mood lifted at the thought of regaining the precious object.

Harriet had one arm firmly around the tree trunk, her body tight up against it, and both her feet on the branch below. She knelt down and reached out an arm. At full stretch her fingers touched the edge of the nest, but she couldn't reach the bracelet. She stretched again, this time moving her body away from the tree a little, but it was no good; she still could not quite reach it.

Then she had an idea. She picked up a loose twig from the top of the nest and used it to hook the bracelet. She raised the twig in the air and watched the bracelet slide down it into her hand, then she moved back closer to the tree trunk. She looked down at Darcey with a great big smile.

Darcey was amazed by her sister's skill and ingenuity. 'Well done, Harriet, that was amazing! Be careful coming down.' She was very eager to finally get hold of the treasure.

Brimming with confidence, Harriet slid down the angled branch like a snowboarder down a slope before passing over the bracelet. Darcey took hold of it firmly. It was warm after being in the afternoon sun.

Chapter 12

Return Home

The sun had now vanished behind the brow of the hill, but it was still warm and the light hung on until late evening at this time of year.

The girls needed to get back and tell their parents about the events of the day. They had ventured quite some way off track in their determination to recover their treasure.

Darcey put the bracelet carefully in her pocket and held it there for extra security. She did not want to lose it again.

They made their way back up the winding path through the gorse; the slope seemed even more precarious than on the way down. At the top of the hill, they looked around. It was warmer than it had been down on the shadowy embankment and there was a lull in the atmosphere; the heart of the day had passed.

Darcey was worried about how long they had been away and if they would find their way back. Her determination to rediscover the lost treasure had distracted them.

After jumping over the stile, they paused for a moment to catch their breath. The field in front of them was now dotted with bunny ears. Lots of small balls of brown fluff were sitting cautiously on the dry grass. The rabbits had come up out of their burrows to feed now that it was cooler.

Matilda tried to count them. 'There are at least twelve,' she guessed.

At that moment, all the bunnies stopping munching. Their ears were up, and their eyes were alert.

Rosie, the family dog, ran through the open gate at the far side of the field, her long ears flapping and her eyes wide with excitement. She playfully chased the rabbits; there were so many that she ran in circles. In truth, she never had a chance to get near any of them, but it was very exciting.

After a quick sniff at several of the burrows, she bounded gleefully to the girls, her tail wagging continuously. She jumped up to Matilda, delighted to see her. Daddy walked up behind her.

'How did you find us?' asked Darcey.

'We've been on the cliff tops the whole time keeping an eye on you,' he smiled.

Darcey was relieved and reassured. 'Look what we have found,' she said, proudly.

Daddy looked carefully. 'Wow, where did you find that? It looks ancient, and it is very beautiful. I think the museum will need to look at it. You must be careful not to break it. Now let's head back. We are having fish and chips with your friends back at the beach before we go back to our holiday house.'

Back at the holiday house, and covered in sand from head to toe, the girls, reflected on their day. They glowed from spending so much time in the sun by the sea. Maybe they could do it all again tomorrow!

Darcey was still buzzing with excitement about her find as she looked out of her bedroom window over the bay. The sun was finally dipping behind the horizon. 'I can't wait to go again tomorrow. We might find more treasure,' she said.

'We might do, Darcey, said Harriet. 'But the real treasure is not the gold we found, it's the time we spend together as a family.'

The girls smiled and hugged, before heading off to bed ready for another long, exciting day tomorrow.

Epilogue

Harriet became a world-famous engineer who built the world's biggest eco-building that was powered by the sun. It had a whole rainforest on top of it and a giant lake below it. She discovered seven new species of plants, birds and animals, and successfully introduced them into the building's rainforest. It was a first for the world's conservation efforts!

 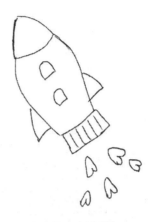

Darcey became a world-famous scientist and worked out how to turn the moon into cheese. She designed a cheese-fuelled rocket to fly there and back so quickly that the journey could be achieved during a school lunch break! She also filmed her own show, *Extinct or Alive*, where she found new species – including the lesser-spotted blue jay.

Matilda won Olympic gold medals for karate seven times; she also won a gold medal for the ski slalom in the winter Olympics. She won *Britain's Got Talent* for her dancing and singing and became an international pop star. She used her newfound fame to raise awareness of the planet and its ecology.

It turned out that the bracelet was not a bracelet at all but an armlet from the Bronze Age, around 1400–1275BC. Similar objects have been found in Ireland and on the Welsh coast. The National History Museum noted the find as official 'Crown Treasure' and gave the children £1,000 each as a reward. Their parents gave them £10 each and put the remaining £990 into long-term savings accounts!

Printed in Great Britain
by Amazon